MICHAEL BOND

Paddington's
NEW ROOM
Illustrated by Barry Wilkinson

One morning, Paddington came down-stairs and found, to his surprise, that everyone else had finished breakfast.

"We have to go out this morning," explained Mrs. Brown, "but we've left you plenty, so you won't go hungry."

"I hope that bear will be all right," said Mrs. Bird, the Browns' housekeeper, as they made their way down Windsor Gardens. "I don't like leaving him on his own for too long."

"I expect he'll find something to do," said Jonathan. "He usually does."

"He was busy writing a new chapter in his scrapbook just before we left," broke in Judy. "I saw the heading. It's called, 'At a Loose End'."

"That," said Mrs. Bird, "is what I'm afraid of."

Mrs. Bird wasn't at all happy about leaving Paddington on his own, especially when he was at a loose end, and had she been able to see over his shoulder at that moment, she would have felt even more uneasy.

Paddington had just started a brand new page.

DECKERATING
MY NEW ROOM

It was called:
DECKERATING MY NEW ROOM.

Paddington's new room was a sore point in the Browns' household. For the time being, he was occupying the guest-room, but Mr. Brown had promised to decorate the attic for him, so that he would have a room he could call his own. For several weeks now, Paddington had had his belongings packed ready for the big move.

For one reason and another, the job had never been started, and now that Paddington found himself left on his own, it seemed a good chance to kill two birds with one stone — decorate the attic *and* do Mr. Brown a good turn into the bargain.

But as he opened the door he nearly fell over backwards in surprise. He'd never seen so many bits and pieces before.

In fact, it was a job to know where to start, and he quite saw why Mr. Brown had kept putting it off.

There was a step-ladder, a table with some rolls of wall-paper on it, two buckets — one full of whitewash and the other full of paste, and several tins of paint, not to mention an electric paint-stirrer.

Paddington decided to test the electric paint-stirrer first, so he opened some paint and switched on the motor.

He wasn't quite sure what happened next, but when he plunged the whirring blades into the tin everything seemed to go dark. It was just as if he were standing in the middle of a hail-storm, except that the flakes were all brown and sticky.

Paddington gazed gloomily around the room. It was a bad start to the day's work.

"Perhaps," he announced, addressing the world in general, "if I do the wallpapering first it will cover all the splashes."

But the wall-paper turned out to be even more of a problem than the paint. As fast as he unrolled one end of the paper, the other end rolled itself up again after him.

And when he tried going the other way
it was just as bad.

So in the end, he decided to start in the middle and work his way outwards with the paste.

At long last, the first piece of paper was ready.

But by that time, it was so heavy with paste, it suddenly fell to the floor, and he found himself left with two very small pieces in his paws.

Heaving a deep sigh, Paddington pressed them into place and then climbed back down again in order to survey his handiwork.

It wasn't very much, but at least it was a start.

And with the help of a broom, he managed to carry on with the rest of the wall.

It was later that morning, while he was having a much needed rest, that Paddington suddenly caught sight of the ceiling.

Seeing how dirty it was, he decided that if he made a good job of whitewashing it, the Browns might not notice the mess he'd made of the rest of the room.

But it was a very high ceiling, and even
when he stood on tiptoe at the top of the
step-ladder, he still had a job to reach it.

Apart from that, he kept having to come down the steps again in order to dip his brush into the bucket, and his fur was starting to go very soggy indeed.

Suddenly, he had a brainwave. The Browns' house was an old one, and in the middle of the ceiling there was a large hook where a big lamp had once hung.

There was also a coil of rope in one corner of the room.

Paddington decided to put two and two together.

He tied one end of the rope to the handle of the bucket of whitewash, then he climbed up the steps and passed the other end through the hook.

It was hard work, because the white-wash was very heavy, but, at long last, the bucket drew level with the top of the steps.

And then, as he took one paw away in order to mop his brow, a strange feeling gradually came over him, rather as if he were floating on air.

It wasn't until his head hit the ceiling
that he realized why.

Everything seemed to happen at once. Before he had time to grab the hook, let alone call out for help, the bucket landed on the floor, and all the whitewash started to run out.

As the bucket became lighter, Paddington felt himself falling.

Half-way down, he passed the bucket
on its way up again.

A moment later he landed with a bump
in the middle of a sea of whitewash.

Even then, his troubles weren't over, for as he tried to stand he let go of the rope and everything went dark again.

But there was worse to come.
Much worse.

When he'd entered the room, he'd come through a door.
He distinctly remembered it.

Now it was no longer there.

Paddington pulled the bucket down over his head again. He felt much safer inside it.

And then the mystery was solved.

"Only a bear like Paddington," said Mr. Brown, "could paper himself up *inside* a room!"

"I think," said Judy, taking hold of Paddington's paw, "you need a hot bath."

"If you don't," said Jonathan, "all that whitewash and paint will set hard."

"And I think," said Mrs. Brown, "we need to get a real decorator in to clear up this mess."

"Hear! Hear!" said Mrs. Bird.

Mr. Brown didn't say what *he* thought.

Paddington went to bed early that night. He had a feeling he was in disgrace.

But, to his surprise, while he was having his cocoa, first Mrs. Brown and then Mr. Brown came in to say good night, and they each gave him some extra bun-money.

Mrs. Bird explained why as she tucked him in for the night.

"Mrs. Brown gave you some extra money because she's getting the room done properly at long last," she said, "and Mr. Brown gave you some because he didn't really want to do it himself in the first place."

"Perhaps," said Paddington, hopefully, "I could decorate your kitchen for you to-morrow, Mrs. Bird?"

Mrs. Bird gave a shudder. "No, thank you," she said firmly. And before Paddington had time to say any more, she gave him some bun-money as well — just to make sure he didn't!

*This story comes from MORE ABOUT PADDINGTON
and is based on the television film. It has
been specially written by Michael Bond
for younger children.*

ISBN 0 00 123337 8 (paperback)
ISBN 0 00 123342 4 (cased)
Text Copyright © 1976 Michael Bond
Illustrations Copyright © 1976 William Collins Sons & Co. Ltd.
Cover Copyright © 1976 William Collins Sons & Co. Ltd. and FilmFair Ltd.
Cover design by Ivor Wood. Cover photographed by Bruce Scott.

Printed in Great Britain